This *LADYBIRD TALE*
belongs to

....

The Ugly Duckling

Retold by Ronne Randall
with illustrations by Polona Lovšin

LADYBIRD 🐞 TALES

ONCE UPON A TIME an old house stood surrounded by fields and woods.

A canal ran past the house, winding gently through the countryside.

Here, in the tall grass on the bank, a mother duck had made her nest.

The mother duck sat patiently on the nest, keeping her eggs warm until they hatched.

She had been sitting and waiting for a very long time. At last, after many days, the eggs began to crack.

One by one the ducklings poked out their heads. "Peep, peep!" they said, as they looked all around. "How big the world is!"

At last all the eggs had hatched, except for one. It was the biggest egg of all. The little ducklings looked at it, waiting for their brother or sister to come out.

Finally the big egg cracked, and out came the last of the chicks. He was very big, and very ugly.

"Oh dear!" said the mother duck. "You don't look like any of my other ducklings. But you're mine, so I'll treat you just like all the others."

The next day was warm and sunny, and the mother duck took her new family down to the canal. She splashed into the water. One by one, the ducklings followed her. Soon they were all swimming beautifully, even the big, ugly one. The mother duck was very proud.

"Quack! Quack!" she said. "Follow me, children. I'll take you to the duckyard."

When they reached the duckyard, the mother duck said, "Walk nicely and stay close to me. And make sure you are polite to that old brown duck over there. She is the most important duck in the yard."

The duckyard was very noisy. The ducklings stayed close to their mother as the other ducks gathered round to look at them.

"Your children are very beautiful," they told the mother duck, "except for that big, ugly duckling."

"Go away! You don't belong here," the ducks quacked at the ugly duckling.

"Leave him alone!" said the mother duck. But the other ducks would not listen.

"He's too big!" they said, pecking at him and biting him.

The ugly duckling was so unhappy in the duckyard that he ran away.

The ugly duckling ran until he came to the great marsh where the wild ducks and geese lived. He hid there in the reeds, trying to rest.

When the wild ducks and geese found him, they asked him what kind of duck he was. The ugly duckling didn't know.

"Well, you're very ugly," they said, laughing at him.

The ugly duckling was frightened in the marsh, so he ran away again. He ran over the fields and meadows, and down a long, winding road.

The wind blew, and the duckling was cold and tired.

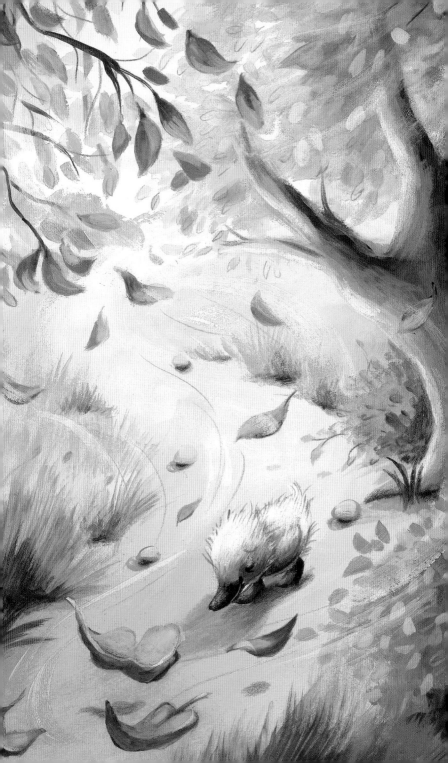

As evening fell, the duckling came to a little cottage. The door was open just a crack, so the ugly duckling was able to creep inside out of the cold.

In the morning, the old woman who lived in the cottage found the ugly duckling.

"You can stay here," she told him, "and we shall have duck eggs."

So the duckling stayed, but he did not lay eggs.

The old woman had a hen that could lay eggs, and she had a cat that could purr.

"Can you purr?" the cat asked the ugly duckling.

"No," said the duckling.

The hen said, "Can you lay eggs?"

"No," said the duckling.

"Then you can't stay here," said the cat and the hen.

So the ugly duckling went away
again. He found a lake where he
could float on the water and dive
to the bottom to find food.

There were other ducks there,
but they all laughed at him
because he was so ugly. The
duckling stayed far away
from them.

Autumn came. The leaves turned brown, and the air grew colder.

One evening, as the sun was setting, a flock of birds flew over the lake. They were handsome white swans with long, graceful necks.

As he watched them, the ugly duckling was filled with a strange longing. He loved the beautiful swans so much that he thought his heart would burst.

Winter came. Snow clouds filled
the sky, and the lake froze.
The duckling had to make a hole
in the ice so he could have a little
space to swim, and water to drink.
He had to keep moving so that
his tiny bit of water wouldn't
freeze over.

At last the ugly duckling was
too tired to swim any more.
He fell asleep, and the ice
surrounded him, freezing him
through and through.

Next morning, a farmer found the duckling.

He put the duckling inside his coat, and took him home to his wife.

The farmer's wife kept the duckling warm, and he soon came back to life.

When the farmer's children saw the duckling, they wanted to play with him. But they frightened the duckling, and he tried to run away from them.

He flew into the milk churn and then landed in the flour barrel. The children laughed and shouted and tried to catch him. The terrified duckling ran away and hid.

All through the long, cold winter, the duckling hid in the reeds of a swamp.

At last springtime came, and sunshine warmed his feathers.

The duckling spread his wings. How strong and powerful they were now!

He flew high into the air, away from the swamp. After a while he came to rest in a gently winding canal.

Three beautiful swans swam towards him.

"They are coming to chase me away," the duckling thought.

But the swans said, "Welcome! Please come and join us."

The duckling looked at his reflection in the water. To his surprise, he was no longer an ugly duckling. He had become a handsome swan!

As he joined the other swans, joy filled his heart.
"I never knew I could be so happy," he thought, "when I was just an ugly duckling."

A History of
The Ugly Duckling

The Ugly Duckling is a literary fairy tale by Danish poet and author Hans Christian Andersen. The story's enduring popularity has meant it has inspired many picture books, musicals, operas and films.

The tale was first published in 1843, along with three other stories in Anderson's collection, *Nye Eventyr. Første Bind. Første Samling* (*New Fairy Tales. First Book. First Collection*). The story quickly received critical acclaim. It was conceived by Andersen and, unlike many fairy tales, does not seem to have been based upon ancient oral stories or traditional folklore.

Following its publication in the 19th century, the story of *The Ugly Duckling* quickly became one of Andersen's best-loved tales, and remains so to this day.

Ladybird's 1979 retelling, written by Ronne Randall, is a classic of its time and helped to bring the story to a new generation.

Collect more fantastic
LADYBIRD 🐞 TALES

Little Red Riding Hood

9781409311126

Goldilocks and the Three Bears

9781409311119

Cinderella

9781409311072

Jack and the Beanstalk

9781409311102

The Gingerbread Man

9781409311096

The Three Little Pigs

9781409311089

The Three Billy Goats Gruff

9781409311065

Hansel and Gretel

9781409311133

Puss in Boots

9781409311225

Rapunzel

9781409311195

Rumpelstiltskin

9781409311164

The Elves and the Shoemaker

9781409311188

Snow White and the Seven Dwarfs

9781409311171

The Enormous Turnip

9781409311218

The Magic Porridge Pot

9781409311201

Sleeping Beauty

9781409311157

The Princess and the Frog

9780718192556

Dick Whittington

9780718192532

The Big Pancake

9780718192549

Beauty and the Beast

9780718192587

The Little Red Hen

9780718192525

The Ugly Duckling

9780718193133

The Princess and the Pea

9780718192570

Chicken Licken

9780718192563

Endpapers taken from series 606d,
first published in 1964

A catalogue record for this book is available from the British Library

Published by Ladybird Books Ltd
80 Strand London WC2R 0RL
A Penguin Company

001

ISBN: 978-0-71819-313-3

Printed in China